For Mum and Dad, for giving me
a childhood filled with happiness - D.D.

For Miska and my parents - N.P.

First published 2022 by Macmillan Children's Books
an imprint of Pan Macmillan
The Smithson, 6 Briset Street, London, EC1M 5NR
EU representative: Macmillan Publishers Ireland Limited
1st Floor, The Liffey Trust Centre, 117–126 Sheriff Street Upper,
Dublin 1, D01 YC43
Associated companies throughout the world
www.panmacmillan.com

ISBN: 978-1-5290-6979-2

Text copyright © Donna David 2022
Illustrations copyright © Nina Pirhonen 2022

1 3 5 7 9 8 6 4 2

A CIP catalogue record for this book is available from the British Library.

Printed in China

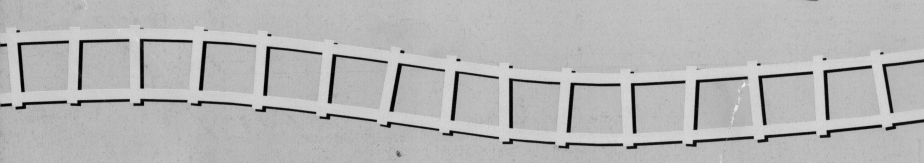

This book belongs to

....

Donna David   Nina Pirhonen

TRAINS TRAINS TRAINS!

Find your favourite!

Macmillan Children's Books

Short trains

1

Long trains

2

Something's gone wrong trains!

3

Steam
trains

Dream trains,
Listen to them puff.

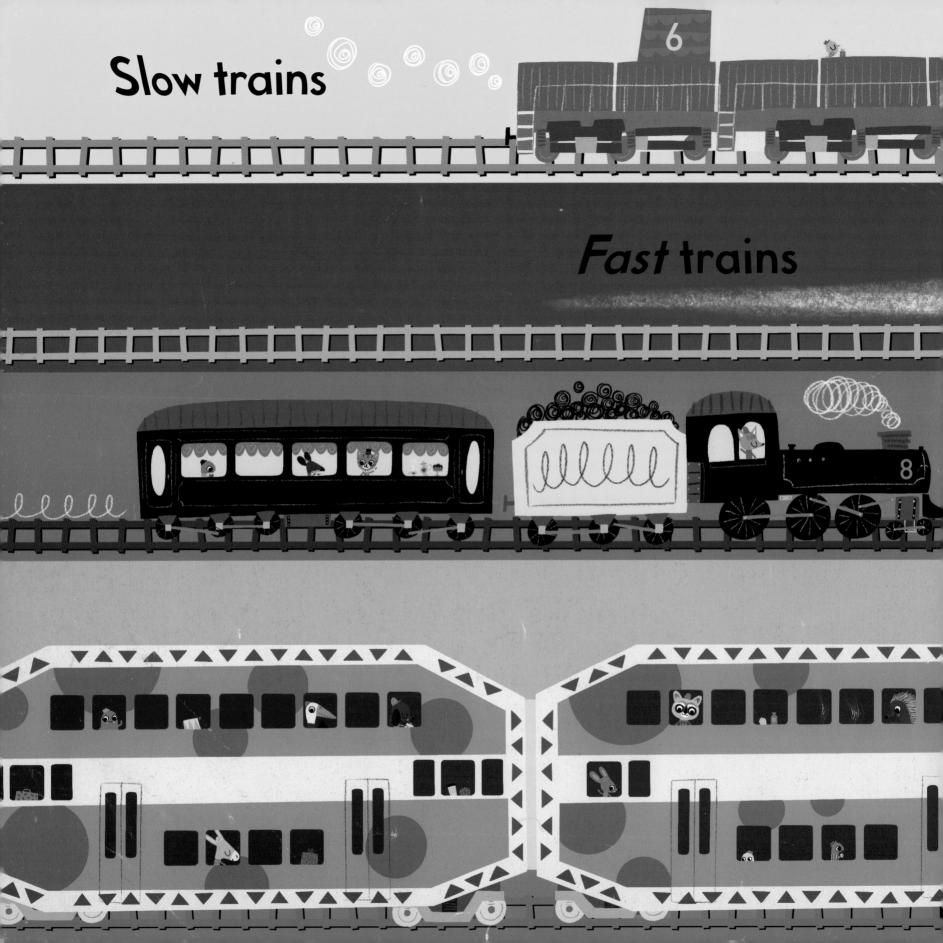

Slow trains

Fast trains

Straight from the past trains

Small **trains**

Big trains, We can't get enough!

Plain trains

Fancy trains

Seat of your pants-y trains

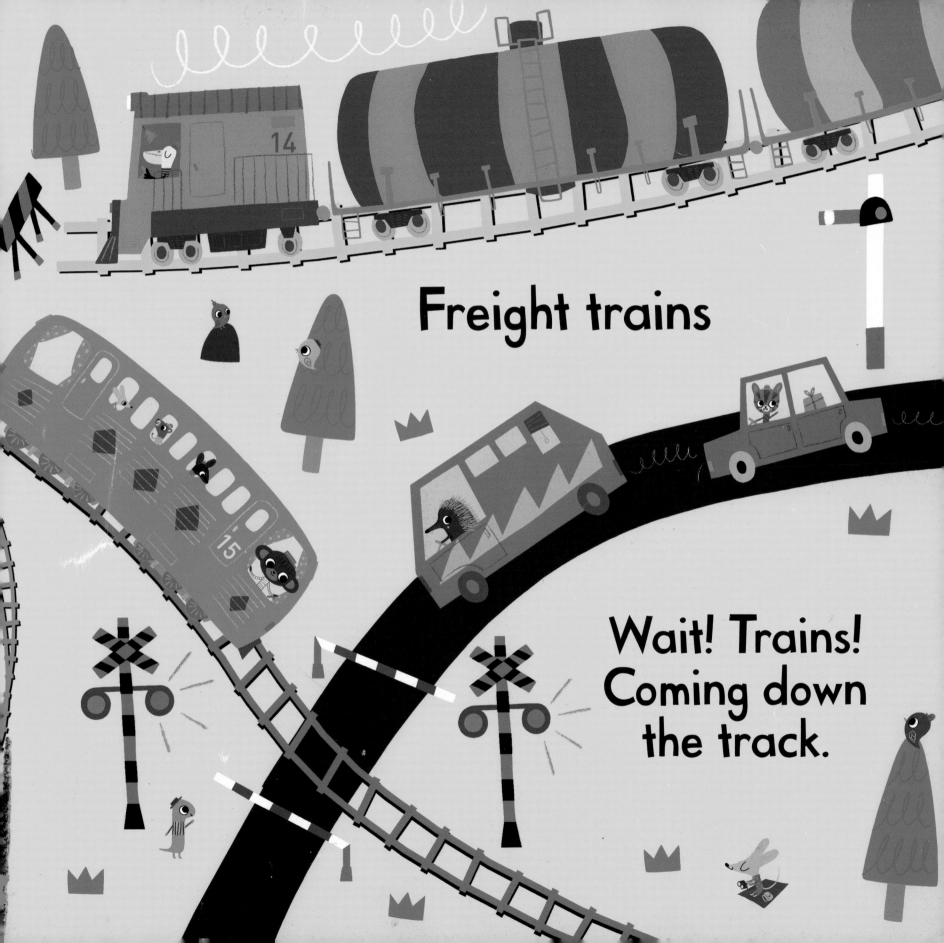

Freight trains

Wait! Trains!
Coming down
the track.

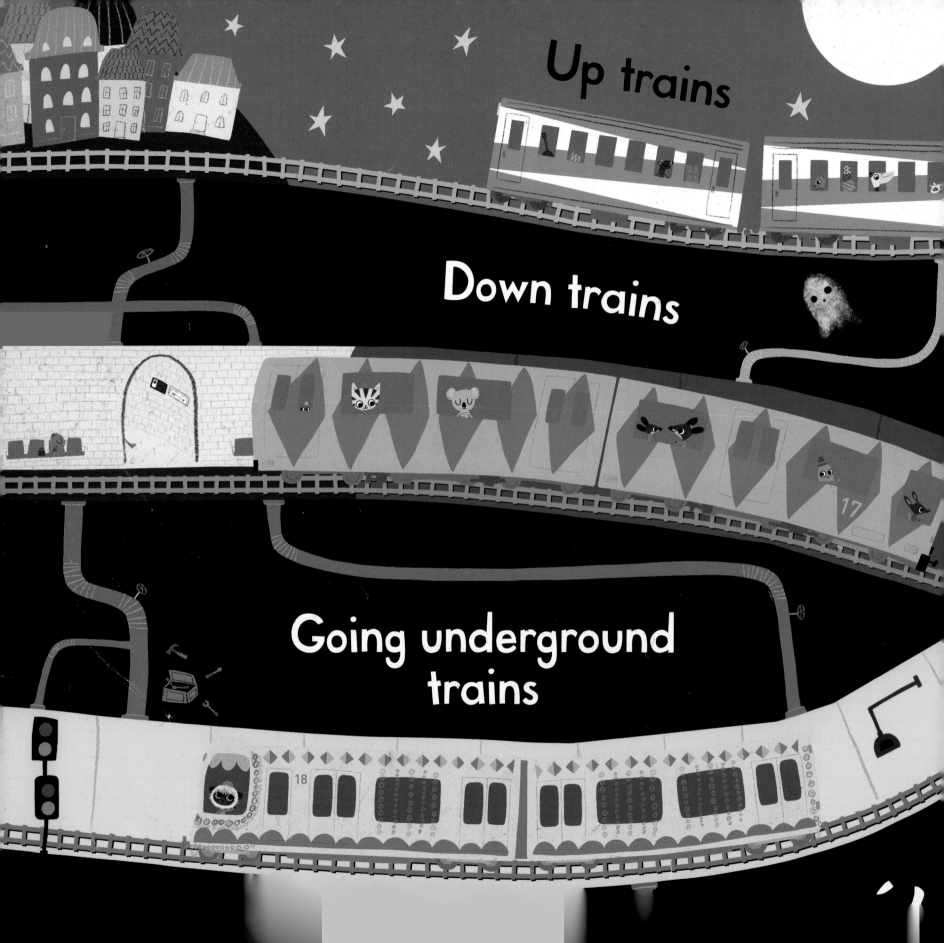

Up trains

Down trains

Going underground
trains

Lost in the dark trains,
Never looking back!

New trains

Old trains

Chugging through
the cold trains

Light trains

Night trains, in a starry sky.

Clean trains

Smelly trains

Shake you up like jelly trains

Quiet trains
Loud trains

Watch them trundle by!

Packed trains

Tea trains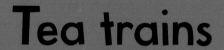

Underneath the sea trains

Quick trains

Slick trains, going *super fast.*

Bullet trains

Rocket trains

Keep them in
your pocket
trains

Hold on really tight trains,
See them flying past!

Red trains

White trains

Rainbow-shining-bright trains

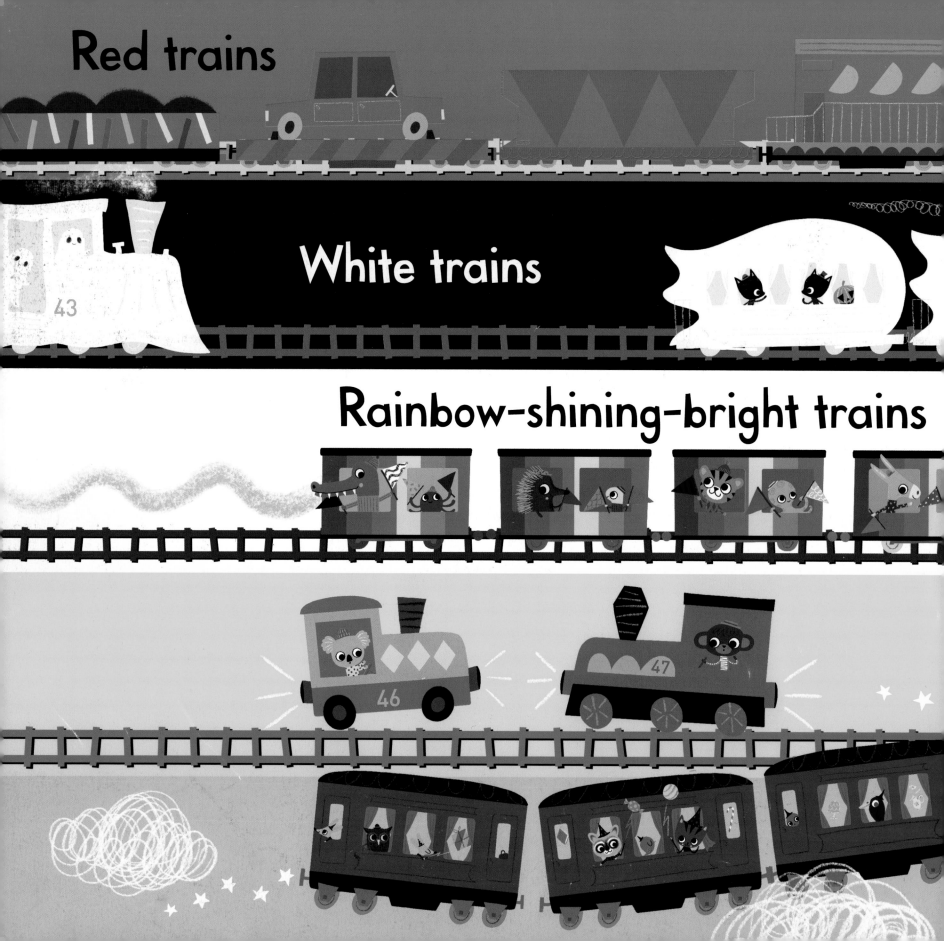

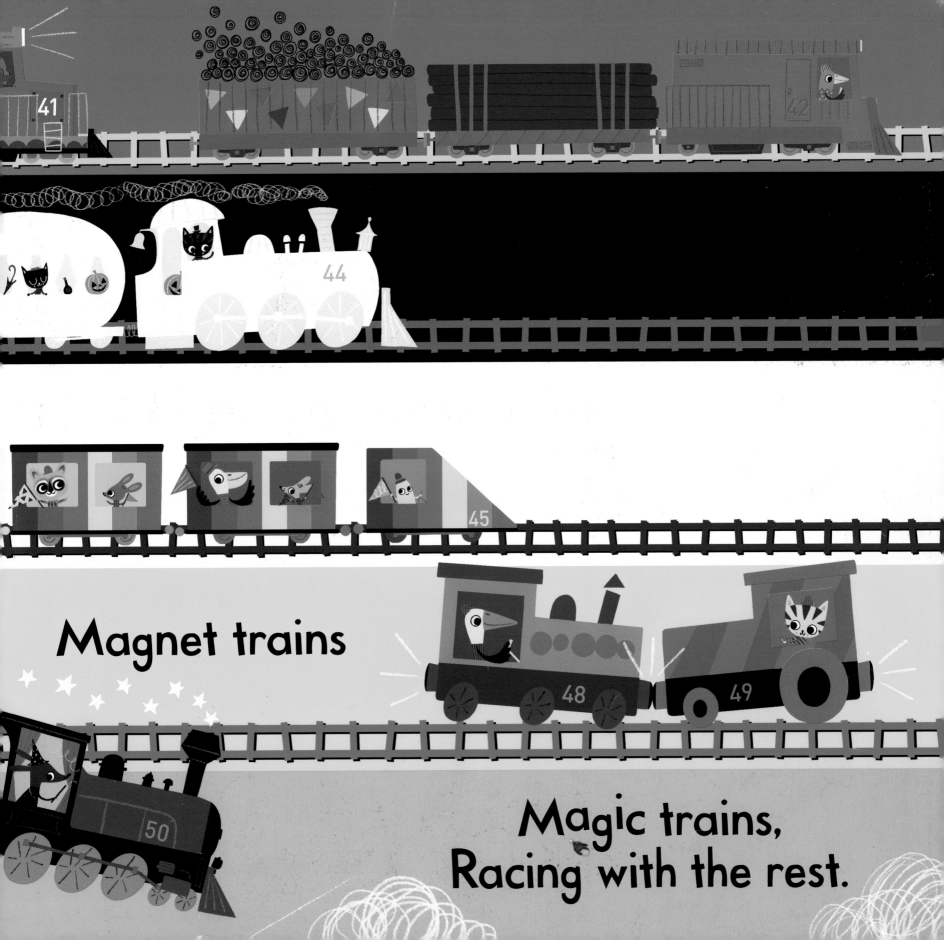

Magnet trains

Magic trains,
Racing with the rest.

Here trains, there trains,
Going everywhere trains!
Try and count them all trains . . .

Which do you like best?

Did You Spot..?

Look back through the book
and see if you can find all these things!

 A pink octopus
(near train number 3)

 A sleepy elephant
(near train number 11)

 A mouse with an ice cream
(near train number 13)

 A blue car
(near train number 15)

A little ghost
(near train number 17)

A skiing cat
(near train number 23)

A duck and her ducklings
(near train number 26)

A turtle family
(near train number 33)

A pair of mice
(in train number 40)

A magical dog
(in train number 50)

What else can you spot?

Reading Together
Tips for Parents and Carers

This book has been specifically created for preschool children. There is plenty of evidence to show that sharing books and reading together helps children to communicate, develop ideas and understanding, and gives them a head start at school. But the most important thing is to enjoy the closeness of sharing a book together.

- You can read *Trains Trains Trains* from start to finish, but you can also **dip in and out** just to look at the pictures.

- The fun, repetitive and rhythmic text **aids language learning and vocabulary.**

- Each train is numbered, to help number recognition and **counting skills.**

- The trains running across the page help your child get used to 'reading' from left to right and **turning the pages of a book.**

- The words and pictures are playful and fun. **Learning through play can be incredibly effective** – your child will be most receptive to new ideas and concepts if they are enjoying themselves.

- Perfect for sharing – reading together is a great way of spending time with your child. It can start new conversations, aid learning, and **develops listening, concentration and vocabulary skills.**

When you read this book together, you could talk to your child about ...

... the numbers on the trains — which ones can they recognize? If they are more confident with numbers, **count along with your child from 1 to 10**, or even up to 50!

... the **words used to describe each train**. Which do they like best? Can your child come up with any more funny or unusual kinds of train?

... their own experiences and opinions. Use the trains in the book as **a starting point for new conversations**. Where would they like to go? How would they get there? What would they see along the way?

... other things they can spot. Try the **'Did you spot'** activity on the previous page. Then try making up your own, choosing different things for your child to find. Can they choose some things for you to spot, too?